Ten Dog Walk

BILL STECKIS

ISBN 978-1-63874-533-4 (paperback)
ISBN 978-1-63874-535-8 (hardcover)
ISBN 978-1-63874-534-1 (digital)

Christian Faith Publishing, Inc.
832 Park Avenue
Meadville, PA 16335
www.christianfaithpublishing.com

Printed in the United States of America

Sammy sits on the edge of the couch
With a sour look resembling a grouch
"I'm bored, and I don't know what to do!"
He was a sad-sounding buckaroo.

Suddenly his head snapped upright,
His eyes widened with pure delight,
His sadness came to quite a crumble
When he heard that familiar grumble.

He knew the sound of the *grrrr, thump, crack*
Could only mean that his dad was back
He eagerly shouted, "HOLY GUACAMOLE!"
It was the garage door raising up slowly.

He ran to the door where his dad comes in
To the house with a brimming, brewing grin.
"What time is it, Dad? Is it six o'clock?"
"Is it time for our special ten dog walk?"

"Ten dog walk?" asked Sam's cool aunt Jo,
Puzzled because she didn't know.
Did she hear it right, was it poppycock?
What in the wide world is a ten dog walk?

Sam thought for a moment about his refrain.
How could he possibly thoroughly explain
What this spectacular special thing was about?
Then he processed it all, and he let it all out.

"It's what we both do to spend time together,
No matter the day, depending on weather.
We walk 'till we see ten dogs in their yards
On our neighborhood streets and boulevards."

"We try for ten, but if we only see
Two dogs while walking or better yet, three,
It's okay, it's still time to walk and wonder
No matter the time frame we might be under."

Dad changed his clothes and Sam put on his shoes.
His dad asks, "What direction do you choose?"
"North, this time." Then they strolled down the block,
Kicking off another ten dog walk.

"Each walk is an adventure, never the same.
Sometimes we are chatty, sometimes we are tame,
But I always will learn something new
By the time each ten dog walk is through."

On this walk right off the bat
Sam said, "Wow, Dad, look at that!"
"Look at that cloud," Sam said with a clamor.
"It looks like Thor, can you see his hammer?"

And then they heard the thunderous spark
Of an Irish setter's booming bark,
As he sprinted toward the chain link fence
In his lavish backyard that was immense.

"Why is he angry and barking at me?"
Sam said, hiding behind a willow tree.
His dad explained, "It is not easy to see,
He's just lonely, like we can all sometimes be."

"Dogs are like people, all shapes and sizes.
Their barks to them are all prideful prizes.
They all have a say no matter their size."
And that is what opened up Sam's green eyes.

"If we treat everyone fairly and listen well
To what they all say no matter how they might tell,
What's in their heart, no matter the tone,
We all just might never feel alone."

Then came a sharp howl from the house just ahead.
It's a Boston terrier whose name is Ted.
He darts right up to the chain-link fence
And his viscous bark grew more intense.

"Why does he do that?" asked Sam on queue.
"That little pooch is scaring me too."
"That is just his job, it's what he is born to do,"
Said his dad. "Protecting his house makes him true blue."

"Look now, he is whimpering and shaking, frail,
And he's gasping quickly while wagging his tail.
He knows you are not a threat to attack,
He probably wants you to scratch his back."

"And you know what else is a good thing?"
Said Sam while standing near a tire swing,
"He is the second dog on this walk, yippee!
And we still have eight more puppies to see."

They walked on and one, two, three
More dogs here and there to see,
Sam then started counting, while taking the lead,
Both noting the color and naming each breed.

"Look, there's a Chow and a coonhound named Holly,
A speckled springer, and a brown and white collie,
A schnauzer named Bowzer, a blue healer named Benny,
And then a golden retriever and a lab named Lenny."

"How do you know all of the multiple breeds,"
Said Sam to his father, "and all of their needs?'
"It's a passion I will never let go of,
Dogs are always willing to give us their love."

"So it's easy to be engaged in what makes them tick
I guess that's why the many breeds, in my mind stick."
"I like dogs too," Said Sam with a lofty endeavor,
"And I think I will like them for ever and ever."

Then in the distance, across the street
They heard the thud of a *bang-bang* beat.
It was a boy hurling a ball as hard as he could,
With anger right into their backyard fence made of wood.

"I know that boy, he's a bully at school,
He is scary and smelly, but kids think he's cool,"
Said Sam hesitantly, in a timid tone.
"But maybe he, like that dog, is alone?"

Sam's dad paused and collected his thoughts,
Knowing Sam's stomach must be in knots
How could he sooth the mind of someone so young?
Then the words tumbled to the tip of his tongue.

"Sometimes there is a reason for such behavior,
We should be kind in the words of our Savior.
I know his dad, and he lost his job
Six months ago. He's my friend named Bob."

"He couldn't pay for baseball fees, it's a bummer
So his son can't play any baseball this summer.
If he acts out and lashes with anger and rage,
It's because he's working through tough things for his age."

"How can we help?" Sam said with a smile
Recalling what he learned just a while
Ago when his dad said to be kind, because
"We should love each other the way Jesus does.

No matter the gesture, right or wrong
His love for us is endlessly strong,
Forgiveness is what he liked to preached,
Endless love is what he loved to teach."

Sam's dad paused and looked to the ground
And then made a "hmm" type of sound.
"Dogs, too, are a shining example of
How to give us unconditional love."

"Think about that lonely Irish setter
When trying to help someone feel better,
To the heart is where you should look.
Don't judge the cover, read the book."

Sam's dad didn't tell, but there was more that he knew,
He continued to marvel as Sam's smile grew.
He said, "Bob is a good man, you could call him swell,
All the people around him know this very well."

"They took up a collection at Bob's work,
And then they got a rare glimpse at a smirk
From Bob as they gave him the money, saying 'cheers,'
For doing a super job for so many years."

Then a quite loud "YES!" came bellowing from
The yard like the banging of a bass drum.
The boy pumped his fist high into the air,
And Sam realized something was happening there.

"Why is the kid now hugging his dad?
I thought he was angry and all sad?"
Sam's dad said, "Looks like his mind is at ease,
He must have used the gift for baseball fees."

"Sometimes just understanding can help
Just like when you hear the big 'ol 'yelp'
Of a dog who's bursting to be good,
He only wants to be understood."

Sam eyes were gazing as he continued learning,
Just as his brain's wheels kept on churning and turning,
He was now hooked on dogs and what their love has brought.
And he put it all together with one great thought.

"It's no wonder God created these creatures
With so many amazing, loving features,
Maybe they are just another way to deploy
How unconditional love can bring so much joy."

Sam's dad's face turned upward gradual and slow
And formed a great smile with a pride and a glow.
As they turned toward home, he said, "Sam, you rock!"
And they headed back home on this ten dog walk.

"We both never know just what we will explore
When we step down the stairs and go out the door.
There is a whole wide world about which to talk
When me and my dad go on a ten dog walk."

About the Author

Bill Steckis is a published author and a long-time television news and sports anchor in Omaha, Nebraska. Bill has coached baseball at the high school and select level for more than twenty years. He conducts the nation's largest free baseball clinic for kids in in Omaha. He is in his third decade of running the free clinic.

CPSIA information can be obtained
at www.ICGtesting.com
Printed in the USA
BVHW050814061221
623326BV00005B/215